Magic Ballerina
Jade and the Surprise Party

Welcome to the world of Enchantia!

I have always loved to dance. The captivating
music and wonderful stories of ballet are so
inspiring. So come with me and let's follow
Jade on her magical adventures in
Enchantia, where the stories of dance will
take you on a very special journey.

p.s. Turn to the back to learn a special
dance step from me...

Special thanks to
Ann Bryant and
Dynamo Limited

First published in Great Britain by HarperCollins *Children's Books* 2010
HarperCollins *Children's Books* is a division of HarperCollins *Publishers* Ltd,
77-85 Fulham Palace Road, Hammersmith, London W6 8JB

The HarperCollins website address is
www.harpercollins.co.uk

1

Text copyright © HarperCollins *Children's Books* 2010
Illustrations by Dynamo Limited
Illustrations copyright © HarperCollins *Children's Books* 2010

MAGIC BALLERINA™ and the 'Magic Ballerina' logo are
trademarks of HarperCollins Publishers Ltd.

ISBN 978 0 00 734876 3

Printed and bound in England by
Clays Ltd, St Ives plc

Magic Ballerina ™
Jade and the Surprise Party

Darcey Bussell

HarperCollins *Children's Books*

To Phoebe and Zoe, as they are the inspiration
behind Magic Ballerina.

Contents

Prologue

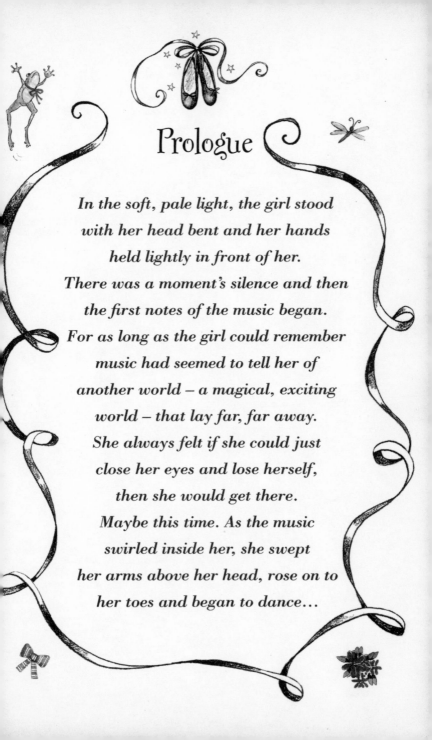

In the soft, pale light, the girl stood
with her head bent and her hands
held lightly in front of her.
There was a moment's silence and then
the first notes of the music began.
For as long as the girl could remember
music had seemed to tell her of
another world – a magical, exciting
world – that lay far, far away.
She always felt if she could just
close her eyes and lose herself,
then she would get there.
Maybe this time. As the music
swirled inside her, she swept
her arms above her head, rose on to
her toes and began to dance…

Working Together

Jade could hear the music in her head. She did a skip kick, a lunge and two quick turns, then she sprung up high, landing in second position. "Yes!" she said, punching the air. "Did you follow what I did? Let's try it together!"

Her partner, Chloe frowned. "Er… can you show me again, Jade?"

Jade looked puzzled. She glanced across at her ballet teacher to see if she was looking in their direction. Madame Za-Za's eyes were on the rest of the class, watching as they made up their own short dances in pairs.

"OK, I'll go back to the beginning. It goes flick, kick, flick, kick, arms up, turn to the right, arms down…" Jade gabbled.

Chloe tried to copy the moves, but she forgot what came after the first arm movements. "Sorry," she said, biting her lip.

Jade tried to hide her disappointment. "Is it that there's too much street dancing in the routine?" she asked. But she didn't wait for Chloe to answer. "I can easily change it. Look, how about *pas de*

bourrée instead of the flick, kicks, like this."

Jade felt excited as she went on making up new steps. Eventually she stopped and turned to Chloe. "Try that."

Chloe took a deep breath, but she'd only just managed the very first bit when

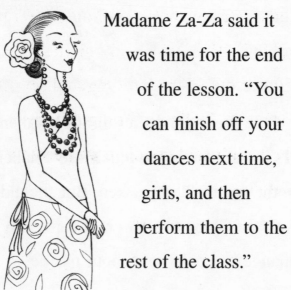

Madame Za-Za said it was time for the end of the lesson. "You can finish off your dances next time, girls, and then perform them to the rest of the class."

Jade didn't even try to hide her disappointment this time. She knew it wasn't Chloe's fault, but dancing in pairs was frustrating. As soon as class was finished, she left the studio, quickly changed out of her red ballet shoes and grabbed her things. Everyone else was chatting away, but Jade didn't feel like talking. "Bye," she said quietly, then slipped out of the building and set off for home, feeling a little guilty that she hadn't said goodbye properly to Chloe.

In her bedroom later that day, Jade put on
her red ballet shoes. She hugged her
knees and stared at the shoes remembering
how they'd come to be hers. She'd found
a parcel posted through her letterbox with

the shoes inside. At first Jade hadn't been sure about ballet dancing and she was still surprised to find that she, Jade Winters, now loved ballet!

And as for the shoes – well they had turned out to be the most special thing of all – not just because they'd brought her to ballet, but because they were magic too. They could whisk her away to the land of Enchantia where all the characters from the ballets lived. There she'd met the White Cat and had such an incredible adventure.

Jade stood up and began to go over the dance she'd made up in the class, but somehow it wasn't working. She tried to hear the music in her head, but it was impossible with her twin brothers and two little sisters making so much noise around the house. There wasn't much room to move in her tiny bedroom either. But in her heart Jade knew that those things weren't the problem. The real problem was with the dance itself. It was just too frantic. Perhaps that was what had made it so hard for Chloe. The steps didn't... flow.

Immediately, Jade set to work, trying to improve the dance. But she'd no sooner got started than her mum called out to ask

her if she'd mind reading her sisters a
bedtime story. "While I bathe the twins,
love."

Jade rolled her eyes, but then felt a leap of excitement as she grabbed a book of fairy tales. She would read them *Sleeping Beauty* and that would remind her of Enchantia.

Her sisters, Lottie and Hannah snuggled up in their beds and listened as Jade began the story. Their eyes grew big and round when she came to the bit about the Wicked Fairy storming into the Princess's christening party in a boiling rage.

"Show us the picture, Jade!" said Lottie.

"Sorry?" Jade blinked a few times, realising that she hadn't been concentrating on the story at all. She'd just been reading the words mechanically while the rest of her brain had been miles away, thinking about Madame Za-Za's.

"Jade! Show us the picture!" This time it was Hannah.

"Sorry." Jade turned the book round so they could see the Wicked Fairy, then went on to read about the Lilac Fairy. She didn't lose concentration now because she loved this part of the story so much. But she didn't get very far.

"Phone, Jade!" came her mum's voice, calling up the stairs. "It's for you!"

Lottie and Hannah frowned.

"I'll be back in a moment," Jade told them as she hurried out of the room.

However, she didn't get downstairs because as she stepped on to the landing her red shoes began to glow. In no time at all the glow turned to a sparkle, and

Jade's heart began to race. *Was this really happening again?* she asked herself excitedly as she was lifted up in a blur of swirling, whirling colours and twinkling sparkles.

The Lilac Fairy

As Jade was set down in a village square
the magical haze cleared and she stared
around her.

"I'm back!" she breathed happily.
"This *is* Enchantia!"

"Jade! Jade!" called a familiar voice.

The White Cat was running up to her. "Lovely day!"

Jade hugged her friend. "It's great to see you again. You look happy, Cat!"

"Well, thank you!" her friend replied with a chuckle, sweeping off his hat in a grand gesture and bowing low. Then he straightened up smartly, leaned forwards and spoke in a low voice. "I think there's er... something rather... odd going on, though, Jade."

"Odd?" said Jade, feeling curious.

"Yes, very odd!" replied the White Cat, looking a bit embarrassed. "You see, I keep coming across people standing in huddles and talking in whispers. But the moment I ask what's going on, they just say, 'Oh nothing!' and leave me none the wiser!"

Jade wrinkled her nose. "That does sound a bit weird," she agreed. And straight after she spoke, as if from nowhere, there was a tiny flash. "Oh! What was that?"

"Exactly!" her friend replied, sweeping the air with his paw. "I *knew* I hadn't been imagining those little flashes I keep seeing! And yet whenever I mention them to anyone, they look at me as though I've gone mad!"

The White Cat shook his head, baffled, and Jade laughed.

A moment later her laughter stopped and her hand flew to her mouth. From out of a hazy mist, before her very eyes, appeared the most beautiful ballerina. And not just any ballerina – it was the one Jade had just been reading about, the Lilac Fairy from *Sleeping Beauty*.

"Hello," said the fairy in a tinkly voice. "I'm Lila."

"Hello… Lila." Jade couldn't help staring at the fairy's sparkling lilac tutu and her beautiful wings that fluttered and shimmered with the palest shades of the rainbow. On her head a diamond tiara sparkled, and in her hand she held a delicate wand.

"Lila, meet Jade!" the White Cat introduced her. Then he turned with concern to the fairy. "What is it, Lila? You look worried."

"We need your help, White Cat. One of the gingerbread children has climbed too high in the tree beside the green, and now she's completely stuck and getting upset."

"Don't worry! I'm on my way!" said the White Cat and he bounded off lightly and quickly.

Jade felt a bit tongue-tied in the presence of the Lilac Fairy, but she didn't need to say anything. Lila had already taken a small step closer and was talking urgently.

"It's true there *is* a gingerbread child up a tree, but she's a very good climber and is only pretending to be stuck so I could talk to you alone."

Jade's eyes widened. "Oh!"

"You see, it's the White Cat's birthday today…"

"The White Cat's birthday! That explains why he looks so happy!"

The date popped into Jade's head. "Oh, but it's the twenty-ninth of February!" She felt a little pang of sadness for her

friend. "Poor old cat only gets a birthday once every four years – whenever it's a leap year."

"Exactly," said Lila. "And because it *is* a leap year this year, we decided we should celebrate it properly. We're going to give him a lovely big party!"

"Cool!" said Jade.

"*But*," said Lila, looking behind her to check he hadn't returned, "it's a surprise. He has no idea!"

Jade smiled. So that was what was going on! "He told me that people keep whispering in little groups and then breaking up as soon as he appears," she said.

Lila's eyes twinkled. "I do hope he doesn't suspect anything because it's going to be wonderful. Practically the whole of Enchantia will be there. And there'll be live music and every kind of dancing, as well as delicious things to eat and drink. At the moment he just thinks he's meeting a few close friends for tea at five o'clock at Little Red Riding Hood's cottage, but when he gets there he'll find a carriage that will whisk him away to the Marshmallow Palace in the Land of Sweets."

Jade felt excitement building up inside her at the thought of such a brilliant plan.

"I'm so glad the shoes brought you here to Enchantia," went on Lila, "because it's practically impossible to get everything prepared for a five o'clock start, without the White Cat finding out. I was wondering whether you could help us."

"Of course!" said Jade. "What can I do?"

"Well, could you distract the White Cat somehow?" Lila frowned in concentration, then broke into a smile. "*I* know! Ask him to show you his favourite old haunts. That'll take him well out of the way!"

Jade nodded. "No problem!"

"Try not to get back until just before five!" added the Lilac Fairy, her face suddenly taking on an anxious look.

"Don't worry, I'll keep him busy!" said Jade, brightly. But she noticed that Lila

still seemed very anxious. "Is… anything the matter?"

Lila sighed. "It's silly, but I just keep worrying that something might go wrong."

"Like what?" asked Jade, puzzled.

"Like King Rat or one of the other wicked characters of Enchantia trying to ruin the party."

Jade shivered. She'd met King Rat before and knew just how horrid he could be. "He hates dancing, doesn't he?" she said quietly.

Lila nodded, looking upset. So Jade tried to cheer her up. "Look, I'm sure everything will be just fine. And the White Cat is going to be over the moon." Then suddenly she remembered something. "You know, I saw a tiny little flash earlier on. And the White Cat says he's seen loads, but no one else seems to know anything about them!"

Lila laughed her light, tinkly laugh. "They're camera flashes. We've hired a photographer called Bettina. I only met her a few days ago, but she's kindly offered to build up a collection of photos so we can show a photo collage to music on a big screen at the White Cat's party." Lila waved to someone behind Jade.

"Ah, here she is now!"

As the lady came closer Lila said, "Bettina, this is Jade. She's going to help distract the White Cat, whilst the preparations for his party are going on."

Bettina nodded at Jade. "Pleased to meet you." She turned to Lila. "And where is the White Cat right now?"

"Rescuing a gingerbread child stuck up a tree!" answered Lila. "At least…"

She was going to explain how this was a bit of a trick, but Bettina was already hurrying off, mumbling about a photo opportunity.

Jade smiled to herself. What a fun visit to Enchantia this was turning out to be. She'd thought at first she'd have to help solve a problem, but all she had to do was explore the place with her friend. Bliss!

The Meeting

"Oh, my shimmering whiskers! It's a while since I've been this way." The White Cat was leaping and bounding along the little path that led to Buttercup Valley.

Jade was hurrying behind trying her

best to keep up with him.

"You're going to love the valley, Jade!" he said, jumping effortlessly on to a boulder at the side and dancing on its smooth surface. "I can't wait to show you the exact spot where I was born!"

Jade secretly felt relieved that her friend had stopped for a moment. It gave her chance to catch up. In his excitement he'd been rushing along so quickly.

He jumped down a moment later, and after a couple of *pas de chats*, he set off again. Jade broke into a jog, so as not to get left behind, and almost crashed into the White Cat. He'd stopped abruptly in

front of a large sign that blocked the
whole lane.

"What's this?" he said, scratching his
head. "Road closed! I don't believe it!"

"Oh dear, does this mean we can't get through to Buttercup Valley?"

The White Cat sighed. "No, it just means we'll have to take a longer route." He shook his head and spoke in a puzzled voice. "It's most odd that this road should be closed, though!"

Together they walked along in silence for a few moments. Jade guessed that her friend was still puzzling over the road being closed, but she was smiling to herself inside. It was obvious why the sign was there. It was all part of the Lilac Fairy's plan to keep the White Cat out of the way for the longest possible time.

"Oh, my glittering eyes!" he said a moment later. "I'd quite forgotten that we have to be back for five o'clock!" He stopped and looked a bit embarrassed. "I haven't said anything, but it's actually my birthday today…"

"Wow!" Jade pretended to be surprised. "Happy Birthday, White Cat!" Then she tipped her head on one side. "I *knew* there was something different about you today!"

"Really?" Her friend smiled then spoke quickly. "Well, Red Riding Hood is holding a small tea party for me at five o'clock. If we're still going to see Buttercup Valley we'll need to hurry. It'll take much longer going this way."

And off they went again. In no time at all, Jade felt herself lagging behind as the White Cat padded along quickly. "One good thing – you'll get to see Swan Lake on this route!" he called over his shoulder.

A bounce came into Jade's step at those words. This was truly amazing. She couldn't believe she'd actually see the real Swan Lake from the ballet. But the bounce didn't help her catch up with the White Cat. He was already way ahead,

even though he'd been putting in a few
high jumps and twirls as he leaped along.

Jade's legs were starting to feel shaky
and she was getting puffed out. "Will I…
meet the swans?" she managed to ask.

The White Cat didn't hear her at first,
he was so far ahead, and Jade had to
force her legs to go even faster as she
repeated her question.

"Absolutely!" came the cheerful reply. Then a serious note came into his voice. "I hope we don't meet the Wicked Fairy, though. She lives close to the lake."

"The Wicked Fairy?" A gasp of alarm came out between Jade's puffs and she stopped so she could catch her breath.

The White Cat must have heard the gasp because he turned round. "Oh, my glimmering eyes!" he said rushing back to her. "You look exhausted. It's my fault! I'm so sorry. I keep forgetting you're only human!"

Jade thought that was quite funny, but she didn't have the strength to laugh. "We

won't… actually meet the Wicked Fairy,
will we?" she asked a little shakily.

The White Cat laid a soft paw on
Jade's shoulder. "No, she's not been seen
for ages. We'll just pass quite near to her
castle, that's all."

Jade nodded. Her friend didn't look
bothered, so there was no need for her to
worry.

They set off again, at a gentler pace,
and the White Cat pointed out the sights –
the Enchanted Wood, Beauty and the
Beast's castle, and way over in the
distance, the tips of the fir trees in the
Land of Snow.

The colour of the sky was subtly
changing from blue to a soft silvery green
colour, when someone approached them
from a little side road.

"Oh, it's Bettina!" said Jade, as the
lady drew closer.

"Bettina?" The White Cat looked baffled. "I thought I knew everyone in Enchantia, and yet here's someone I've never met before!" He threw a questioning glance at Jade. "When did *you* meet her?"

But Bettina had come right up to them by then, and was shaking the White Cat's paw.

"Hello, there!" she said in a friendly but business-like voice. "I'm a photographer and I'm building up a collection of animal images. I wonder if you'd mind posing for me." She threw a quick smile at Jade, and Jade grinned back. She obviously wanted another shot of the White Cat for the special collage. It was so clever of Bettina to invent a story about animal photos. "Perhaps the two of you would be good enough to stand over here by this tree," Bettina said, lining up her camera.

"Well, I'm not sure…" the White Cat began to say. Jade was surprised that he sounded so wary. And he didn't look himself, either. He seemed agitated, jumping from foot to foot and frowning deeply.

"It's all right," she said in a whisper. "I met Bettina earlier when I was with the Lilac Fairy."

But the White Cat stayed put and Jade felt a little embarrassed that he wasn't helping.

"Are you from round these parts?" he called out to Bettina.

She waved her hand towards Swan Lake. "Yes, my house is over there. I don't get out much though. I've been rather... ill."

"Oh dear," said Jade loudly, when the White Cat didn't reply. "I'm sorry to hear that, Bettina." Jade turned to her friend and spoke in a hiss. "Whatever's the matter, White Cat?"

"Something doesn't add up," he

whispered. "If you met her when you were with Lila, how has she managed to get all the way back here *before* us?"

Jade had to agree it was odd, but it didn't really matter, did it?

"She only wants to take our picture then we can move on."

The White Cat grunted and got into position by the tree trunk, but Jade couldn't help noticing that he wasn't smiling.

"Say cheese!" Bettina instructed in a sing-song voice. And a second later there was a flash.

Suddenly Jade couldn't move. Oh no! The White Cat had been right to be suspicious. She and the White Cat had been turned into statues!

Imprisoned

With a nasty cackle Bettina whirled around in a storm of black sparks. Then she transformed into an ugly old hag wearing a ragged grey dress.

Jade might not have been able to move, but she could still see and hear. Her heart felt as though it was banging against her ribs as she realised who must be standing before her. It was none other than the Wicked Fairy herself.

"Ha! That'll teach the lot of you!" the Wicked Fairy snapped in a scratchy voice. "It is *very* rude to organise big parties and leave certain people off the guest list."

Jade felt sorry for the White Cat. The Wicked Fairy's words must have made no sense to him. After all, as far as *he* knew, he was only going to a small tea party.

The fairy raised her wand. "I shall release you from my spell once midnight

passes and this *special birthday*…" she

snarled at the White Cat, "…is no more!"

She waved the wand, closed her eyes and
chanted:

*"With a wham, a gazzam and a crash,
take them to the tower!*

*With a wham, a gazzam and a flash,
until the darkest hour!"*

Then there was a sound like a mighty
cymbal crashing, and a flash like lighting.

Jade found herself sitting beside her
friend in a tall, dark tower room, with her
back against a cold wall. Thank goodness
they weren't statues any more. But being
imprisoned seemed almost as bad.

"White Cat..." she said slowly as she turned her head.

The White Cat reached out a paw and held Jade's hand. "You didn't get to see the swans," he said sadly.

"And you didn't get to show me where you were born," Jade added with a sigh. Then she turned to her friend, her eyes round and sorrowful. "I'm so sorry. I shouldn't have encouraged Bett… I mean the Wicked Fairy to take the photo. It's my fault that we're prisoners, and you're going to miss your…" Jade stopped mid-sentence. Somehow it seemed wrong to spill the beans about the wonderful surprise party, even though her friend wouldn't be able to go to it now.

The two of them sat there in their own little worlds. Jade's brain was racing. If only there was a way to escape. She glanced up at the window at the very top of the tower, but it was too high up for them to think about getting out that way.

The White Cat must have followed her gaze. "If you stand on my shoulders," he said thoughtfully after a moment, "at least you'd be able to see Swan Lake."

"Well, that's something," said Jade.

A moment later she was peeping out of the window. The most beautiful lake lay in the distance. "Oh wow!" she breathed.

"It's so calm and I can see the swans too – lots of them, snowy white and as graceful as ballerinas! And…" Jade broke

off her excited chatter when a ball of
green smoke came billowing up and
blocked her view.

"What's going on?" coughed the White
Cat. "Is there a fire?"

Jade didn't reply. She just stared down.

The smoke was clearing to reveal the Wicked Fairy climbing into a black carriage. Two rats were tied to the front of the carriage.

"Get going, you pathetic beasts!" yelled the Wicked Fairy as she lashed the reins then waved her wand, her voice rising to a screech.

"*With a wham, a shazzam and a flash,
take me to the square!*

*Bettina will snap the people, and make
them stop and stare! Ha ha ha!*

Then the carriage disappeared in a puff
of green smoke.

Jade clambered down from the White Cat's shoulders. "Oh, White Cat, did you hear that? The Wicked Fairy is going to pretend to be Bettina again, and trick everyone just like she tricked us!" Jade's voice was trembling. "She's going to turn them all into statues! We've got to stop her!"

The White Cat had been shaking his head in despair when suddenly he sprung up, full of life. Jumping into the air, he criss-crossed

his ankles six times before landing lightly and breaking into a grin. "I've got it!"

"What?"

"The answer! There's a special dance that can be performed to summon the swans. I don't know why I didn't think of it before."

"You mean you can do this dance and the swans'll fly here to rescue us?" Jade could feel her excitement mounting. At last, a ray of hope.

"Well… almost," said the White Cat. "But the trouble is, cats can't do bird dances in Enchantia. The magic won't work. But I can teach *you* how to do the

dance! And *you* can summon the swans!"

Jade felt her hope dissolving a little. What if she couldn't manage the dance? But then she jutted out her jaw. She had to at least give it a try. "OK, Cat!" she said firmly. "Show me how it goes!"

The White Cat raised his arms slowly through first position to fifth then opened out to second. Jade copied him, so far so good. But then his feet began a series of complicated steps and Jade gulped.

"Can you show me that bit again, please?" she said.

The White Cat repeated the sequence and went on a little further. "OK? Got

that?" He carried on moving through the
steps as he talked, and in the end Jade
was in a complete muddle.

"Sorry, White Cat," she said in a small
voice. "I can't keep up when you go so
quickly."

"No, no, my fault entirely! I must learn to slow down!"

But the next time he showed Jade the steps, he went just as fast. "There! Got it now?"

Jade shook her head miserably.

"No, no! My fault again. Absolutely! Right, one step at a time."

A few minutes later, after a great deal of concentration, Jade thought she had finally learned the steps. She took a deep breath then stood right in the centre of the tower. Waiting until she could hear the music inside her head, she began to dance.

In no time at all, the music grew louder

and Jade was dancing with all her heart.

As she sank into the final position, with

her arms softly crossed at the wrists, she

heard a noise from outside the window. A flapping of wings.

"You've done it! They're here!" cried the White Cat.

Jade looked up and gasped. A white swan had alighted on the stone window ledge. And against the blue sky she could see the beating wings of another swan just behind.

"Sabrina! Sahara!" the White Cat called. "We're in here!"

The Land of Sweets

The ride on the back of the swans was
magical. Jade was on Sahara's back, and
the White Cat was on Sabrina's. The
Land of Enchantia lay beneath them like
a patchwork quilt as the two swans glided
smoothly through the bright sky.

The church clock was just striking five as they were set down outside Red Riding Hood's cottage. Jade and the White Cat thanked the swans and waved them off as they flew back to their distant lake.

The White Cat was staring around. "It's very quiet," he said, his brow furrowed.

Jade's heart fluttered with worry when she thought about what the Wicked Fairy

could have done. What if Red Riding
Hood and all the guests were statues? She
looked at the White Cat's grave face and
guessed he was thinking the same thing.

Without a word they made for the front
door. But they'd hardly taken a step when
a loud noise pierced the silence.

They turned round to see a black
carriage, pulled by two rats, hurtling
round the bend.

"Quick!" cried the White Cat. "Don't
let her see you!"

He pulled Jade down behind the fence
around Red Riding Hood's cottage and
seconds later the carriage thundered past.

Jade couldn't help peeping over the top and caught a glimpse of the Wicked Fairy's scrawny neck and pointed chin. Her face was screwed up in a look of triumph. "Ha! My work here is done! Take me home, Rats. I can't wait to tell my prisoners!"

Jade felt a shiver run down her spine as she and the White Cat slowly straightened up and looked at each other despairingly.

"What do you think she meant about her work being done?" Jade asked in a small voice, although she knew the answer already. "She's turned everyone into a statue, hasn't she?"

The White Cat nodded glumly, but then suddenly sprang into action. "We have to find the Lilac Fairy. It's our last hope. She's the only one with enough magical powers to bring the statues back to life."

"Right," said Jade, catching some of her friend's energy.

Together they hurried to Lila's cottage.

But there was no sign of her.

Of course! thought Jade, *She'll be in the Land of Sweets, getting ready for the party. But how I can tell the White Cat that without giving the game away?*

"Er… actually," she began hesitantly, "I think I remember Lila saying something about visiting the Land of Sweets this afternoon."

A spark of hope came into the White Cat's eyes. "In that case," he replied, "get ready to jump into the magic ring!"

He swished his tail in a glittering circle and it lifted them both up in a billow of sparkles.

A moment later they were standing in the Land of Sweets.

Now where is the Marshmallow Palace?
Jade thought. She needed the White Cat's
help. She didn't want to give anything
away, but this was more important.

"Er, Lila mentioned a palace or a grand
mansion or something. I'm afraid I can't
remember the name of it, though."

"Oh, right," said the White Cat,
knitting his eyebrows. "Let me see, was it
the Grand Palace?"

Jade shook her head.

"The Chocolate Palace?"

"No..."

"The Marzipan Mansion?"

"I don't think so..."

"The *Marshmallow Palace*?"

Jade detected a glint in the White Cat's eye. "Yes, that was it! The Marshmallow Palace!" she said.

"My favourite," he said, whipping his tail around smartly. "Let's be on our way!"

They were set down only seconds later right outside the Marshmallow Palace. And now Jade had another problem. If the White Cat went inside he would see the party preparations. And he was already marching on ahead.

81

"Er… White Cat, I think one of us should stay here and watch out for the Wicked Fairy!" she gabbled. "It would be awful if she came back. I'll go and look for Lila."

The White Cat looked a bit confused, but Jade rushed past him and into the palace before he could protest.

The grand reception hall had already been decorated with hundreds of white and gold balloons. Over the door to the ballroom, in giant gold letters it said *Happy Birthday, dear White Cat*.

Jade wished she had time to appreciate it, but she had to find Lila as quickly as possible. Pushing back the door to the

ballroom, she could hardly believe her eyes. The ceiling sparkled, the walls glittered, the floor gleamed and the pillars glistened. There were buttercup garlands and streamers of daisy chains everywhere. But that wasn't all. Amongst the splendour was something that sent a shiver down her spine…

There stood a hundred silent statues.

Wands at Work

Jade tiptoed round despairingly, searching for the Lilac Fairy. She knew in her heart of hearts that Lila would probably be a statue too, but she was trying to hold on to the hope that she might be wrong. As she walked forward, she remembered

what the Wicked Fairy had said – that she would release Jade and the White Cat once his birthday was over. That meant she had probably been intending to break the statue spell too. Jade swallowed. What would happen now? The Wicked

Fairy would get in a terrible rage when she returned to her castle and discovered that her prisoners had escaped. She would definitely want revenge. And what better revenge than to refuse to break her spell so the people of Enchantia remained as statues forever?

Jade was close to tears when she found Lila's statue. She looked sorrowfully into her eyes. But what she saw there, made her snap out of her despairing mood and jump to attention. The Lilac Fairy was trying to tell her something. What was it? Jade tried hard to pick up the message.

"There *is* something I can do... Is that

what you're trying to tell me, Lila?" she
asked shakily.

Lila's eyes seemed to glitter. Jade knew
she'd understood correctly. But what
could the Lilac Fairy want her to do? She
thought back to the dark tower where

she'd been imprisoned so recently. How had she escaped? By doing a special dance to summon the swans. That was how Enchantia worked. Of course!

Jade racked her brains to think what dance she should do…

"The Lilac Fairy's dance from *Sleeping Beauty*! Could that be it?"

Lila's eyes were glittering even more. But Jade's excitement came crashing down as she realised something.

"Oh, Lila," she said with a deep sigh. "I can't do your dance. I don't know the right steps."

Still Lila's eyes glittered with hope.

Across Jade's mind flitted the image of the Lilac Fairy from her book of *Sleeping Beauty* at home. She could visualise the exact ballet position that the fairy held in the picture. Maybe if she tried to imitate it…

She concentrated with all her might, raising her arms into fifth position. Then she extended her leg into an *arabesque*, taking care to point her toe.

The fairy was on pointe in the picture, but Jade hadn't started pointe work yet, so she rose on to demi-pointe. It was so hard to keep her balance. She met Lila's eyes again and they were really sparkling.

Nothing was happening, though. She tipped her head the slightest bit to frame her face perfectly. Still nothing happened. She softened her wrists. And in that

instant there was a flash of gold and the Lilac Fairy moved.

Jade clasped her hands. "Oh! You've come back to life!"

"Yes," replied Lila, leaning forwards and dropping the lightest kiss on Jade's cheek. "Thanks to you!"

It was the most wonderful moment to enjoy, but the other people of Enchantia still needed to be freed.

"There's no time to lose!" said Lila. "First I need to release all the fairies so they, in turn, can release everyone else!"

As she was talking she flew around the ballroom, tipping her wand lightly on each of the fairies' heads. One by one they began to move again. Lila smiled as she watched her fairies flitting round. "It takes more than a spell from a wicked old fairy to stop *this* surprise party happening!" she said, her tinkly laughter blending with a ballroom *full* of cheers as statue after statue came back to life.

Jade had a shock when she saw that Red Riding Hood was actually there in the ballroom too.

"I was just about to set off on my way home," the young girl told her anxiously, "when the Wicked Fairy came crashing in and turned us all into statues."

"So there's no one at your house?" Jade asked her.

"No one at all." Red Riding Hood shook her head and looked around. "So where's the White Cat?" she asked fearfully.

"Oh! I'd quite forgotten," said Jade, clapping her hand to her mouth, "he's outside! He might come looking for me at any moment! I haven't said a word about the party. He still thinks he's going to your house for tea!"

"Quickly, go outside and ask him to magic you both back to Red Riding Hood's cottage then," said Lila. "I'll meet you there!"

Jade didn't need telling twice. Rushing

outside, she went straight to the White
Cat.

"What took you so long?" he started,
but he didn't have a chance to finish as
Jade interrupted him. "I found Lila, White
Cat. Everything's all right. I'll explain
later. Lila says we should go to Red

Riding Hood's house now – there isn't a moment to lose!"

"But what about all the statues?" asked the White Cat. "Is everyone OK?"

"They're safe. Lila's seen to that," said Jade vaguely. "So can you magic us to Red Riding Hood's cottage?"

The White Cat looked at Jade as though she was mad. "But…"

"That's what Lila told me to ask you," she said firmly.

The White Cat shook his head in confusion. "Well if that's what Lila said…"

A few moments later they were set down outside Red Riding Hood's cottage. Jade gasped at the sight of the magnificent golden carriage, standing there in front of them.

Lila stepped forward and held out her hand to the White Cat.

He was still wearing a bewildered look. "How did you get here ahead of us? What exactly's going on and where is everyone? What's happening!"

"A party," replied Lila, smiling.

"I know about that," said the White Cat. "Red Riding Hood's been expecting me. But what about all my friends? Are they safe?"

"They are indeed," said Lila. "But not here. They're waiting with Red Riding Hood in the Land of Sweets."

"Waiting for who?" The White Cat let go of Lila's hand and made to go towards the cottage. But Jade stopped him.

"Look Cat, please do as Lila says. Here is your carriage."

The White Cat stared at the glittering carriage. "Are you sure? For me?" he asked faintly.

Lila and Jade both nodded and grinned at each other as they opened the door for their friend.

The Surprise

"Oh, my shimmering tail! A surprise party! This is unbelievable!" cried the White Cat as he stared at the sign above the door to the ballroom. Then he turned with shining eyes to Jade. "Did you know about this?"

Jade grinned. "Yes!"

"And you kept it a secret!"

Jade giggled. "It wasn't easy!"

The White Cat patted her arm with his paw and skipped into a graceful *pas de chat* as Lila flung open the door to the ballroom. The loudest claps and cheers rang out, filling the whole palace.

"Oh, my glittering whiskers!" the White Cat exclaimed, which made everyone cheer all the more loudly. Then they broke into song and Jade sang too at the top of her voice.

"Happy Birthday, dear White Cat. Happy Birthday to you!"

"I am such a lucky fellow!" declared
the White Cat pirouetting round and
greeting all his guests. "What a wonderful
surprise."

It was the best party Jade had ever attended. As everyone tucked into the most lavish feast, she told her friend the story of all that had happened. She began with Lila asking for Jade's help in keeping him out of the way of the party preparations. And she ended with the moment when she'd managed to bring the Lilac Fairy back to life.

"I'm very proud of you!" declared the White Cat. "And I'm so relieved that everything has turned out perfectly! Would you do me the honour of dancing with me?"

"As long as you let me keep up with

you!" Jade replied, laughing a little nervously.

"Then why don't *you* lead and I'll try to follow!" suggested the White Cat.

Everyone clapped in time as the two of them twisted and turned, twirled and jumped.

There were no celebratory photos now

that Bettina was gone, but that really didn't matter.

"Oh, your sparkling shoes!" the White Cat cried out finally.

At first Jade thought it was just another of his outbursts. But then she realised he was looking down at her red shoes, and saw that they really were glowing.

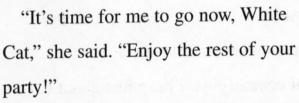

"It's time for me to go now, White Cat," she said. "Enjoy the rest of your party!"

The White Cat held both her hands in his paws. "Thank you for everything! This party is the best ever!"

Jade smiled as she let go of his paws and felt herself being lifted up in a swirling mass of bright colours. "Goodbye! Goodbye!"

Next thing she knew, Jade was standing on her landing at home just outside her sisters' room.

"Are you coming, Jade?" came her mum's voice from downstairs.

Of course! She'd been just about to go to the phone when the shoes had whisked her away. And as usual when she returned from Enchantia, no time at all had passed in the real world.

She took the

phone from

her mum.

"Hello?"

"Oh, hi Jade.

It's Chloe."

"Chloe!" Jade suddenly

felt ashamed of the way she'd been in

class that morning. The White Cat's voice

popped into her head. *I keep forgetting

you're only human*! And she began to

apologise down the phone. "Sorry about

this morning, Chloe. I shouldn't have

gone so fast. I know how hard it is when

you can't keep up. I'm really sorry."

"It's OK," Chloe replied, sounding happy. "I was phoning to ask if we could get together during the week and have a practice?"

"Yes, that would be great!"

When Jade put the phone down she went back upstairs and into Lottie and Hannah's room, ready to finish off *Sleeping Beauty*. She stopped in the doorway, though. Both her sisters were fast asleep.

Jade crept in and picked up the book.

She turned straight to the page with her favourite picture and studied it carefully.

What a beautiful pose the Lilac Fairy was holding. Jade closed her eyes and saw a picture of herself in the ballroom of statues. Then she opened her eyes and smiled. She'd had such an amazing adventure. She couldn't wait to go on many more.

Pas Couru

Imagine you are trying to keep up with the White Cat by moving swiftly and gracefully across the stage...

1.
Start in a *demi-plié* with your right leg extended in front of you and your foot pointed in front. This is called a *pas degage*. Hold your arms curved in front of you in first position.

2.
Transfer your
weight to your
right leg and glide
into a light run on
demi-toes.

3.
Move with tiny
steps and
imagine you
are floating
through a mist.
Your arms can
be raised or
low but must
be consistent
throughout.

4.
Finish your run
gracefully and
comfortably come
down on your
right foot with left
foot pointed in
front.

Precious things are going missing in
Enchantia. Is someone up to no good?

Read on for a sneak preview
of Jade's next adventure…

Jade's feet touched solid ground once more, and she stared straight ahead in amazement. Before her stood a grand, majestic palace. The sun's rays made its white marble walls gleam brightly and the tall pointed spires glistened against the blue sky.

It was hard for Jade to take her eyes off such a magnificent sight. Jade smiled as she shielded her eyes from the sun with her hand and looked around for her friend, the White Cat. Any moment now he would come bounding up to her. He always did.

"Ah, here he is…"

But Jade was mistaken. The person approaching her was a fine, upright lady dressed in a long full skirt and a cloak. *She probably works at the palace*, thought Jade. Maybe she's a lady-in-waiting.

"Hello, my dear. What has happened to your beautiful scarf?"

Jade was surprised that the lady had stopped to

talk to her. She'd somehow seemed a bit snooty, walking along with her nose in the air. And it was an even bigger surprise when she began to examine the silver scarf that Jade was still clutching.

"Very pretty, my dear. Very pretty indeed. But look, a thread has come loose. Do you see?"

"Sorry? What?" Jade hadn't been paying attention. She'd been looking round, wondering where the White Cat had got to. She wasn't all that bothered about a little thread coming loose, but politely she looked at the scarf.

"Oh yes," she replied distractedly.

"I can mend it for you…"

"No, it's fine, honestly." Jade turned her head this way and that. Surely the White Cat would be here very soon.

"No, my dear, I'm afraid it's not fine," the lady started again. "You see, the scarf will unravel completely if left with this loose thread hanging. Let me take it and mend it for you. I can do it very quickly."

"Er…"

"I can bring it back in an hour. Meet me here outside the palace. How does that sound?"

"Oh… OK."

Jade really didn't mind one way or the other whether the scarf got mended. All that mattered was that her friend turned up to greet her. "OK, well, thank you very much."

And before she knew it, the lady had turned on her heel and was walking away.

Jade looked round again, and this time her heart lurched with happiness as she saw the White Cat bounding towards her, a big grin on his face.

To be continued…

The Story of Sleeping Beauty

Everybody at the royal palace was excited.
The King and Queen were having a big
christening party for their baby daughter –
Princess Aurelia. "Make sure everybody in the
kingdom is invited," the King told his servants.

"Especially all the fairies," added the Queen.
"They are Aurelia's godmothers."

On the day of the party the fairies arrived
wearing their prettiest dresses. They leaned
over the little Princess's cradle and gave her
their special presents.

"I give you the gift of happiness," said the first fairy.

"I give you the gift of beauty," said the next. One by one the fairies whispered their magical gifts. But just as the last fairy was about to speak a crash of thunder shook the palace and a horrible, ugly old fairy appeared.

"It's the Wicked Fairy, Carabosse," gasped the frightened Queen.

"What do you want?" asked the King, trying to sound brave.

"You didn't invite me to the party," snarled Carabosse. "Now you'll be sorry."

Before anyone could stop her she waved her wand over baby Aurelia. "When the Princess is sixteen years old," she cackled, "she will prick her finger on something sharp and die!"

Just then the Lilac Fairy stepped forward. "I haven't given Aurelia my gift yet," she said gently. "I can't undo the evil spell, but I can change it. The Princess will not die. She will

sleep for a hundred years. Then the spell can be broken by the first Prince who kisses her."

Carabosse was very angry the Lilac Fairy had spoiled her spell and she stormed out of the palace. But the King and Queen were grateful that their daughter had been saved.

The years passed and Aurelia grew up into a lovely, happy girl. On her sixteenth birthday she had a big garden party. Lots of people came, including four handsome Princes who all wanted to marry her. The Princess had a lovely time, dancing with the Princes, but she didn't fall in love with any of them. Near the end of the party an old lady wearing a long dark cloak offered the Princess a bunch of flowers.

"Happy Birthday," she croaked.

Princess Aurelia had very nice manners so she said thank you, and took the flowers. But as she held them, something pricked her finger.

"Ouch," she said in surprise, then promptly fell fast asleep. The old lady was really the Wicked Fairy. She had tricked Aurelia by hiding something sharp, called a spindle, in the flowers.

The sleeping Princess was carried inside, up the spiral staircase and tucked into her big bed. But the Queen could not stop crying.

"My poor daughter," she sobbed. "When she wakes up in a hundred years she will be all on her own."

The Lilac Fairy had an idea. She flitted
through the palace sprinkling fairy dust. Before
long everybody in the palace had fallen asleep.
The cooks fell asleep with their faces in
puddings, the guards fell asleep and banged
their metal helmets and in Aurelia's bedroom
the King snored loudly, curled up on the floor.
All around the palace a huge forest began to
grow. It was so deep and full of brambles
no one ever went there. The years passed and
everybody forgot about the palace and the
beautiful sleeping Princess.

Exactly one hundred years later a young Prince was wandering along the edge of the dark, silent woods. "I wonder what's inside," he thought.

"I can show you," said a soft voice.

The Prince was startled when he looked up and saw the Lilac Fairy and her friends floating among the trees. "Look," they told him and waved their magic wands. Suddenly Princess Aurelia appeared dancing between the fairies. She was the most beautiful girl the Prince had ever seen. But when he stepped forward to dance with her she disappeared.

"The real Princess is under a spell," the Lilac Fairy explained. "You can save her if you are brave enough to go through these woods."

At once the Prince drew his sword and stepped between the trees.

As the Prince got deeper into the forest he heard an ugly laugh. An angry fairy stood in his path. "Turn round and go home," shrieked

Carabosse, pulling her scariest face. But the Prince waved his sword at her and frightened *her* away. Nothing would stop him from finding the beautiful Princess.

At last he reached the palace. He pushed open the creaking doors, tiptoed through the cobwebby halls, and climbed the spiral staircase to where Aurelia was sleeping. He kissed her gently and Aurelia instantly woke up. They fell in love at once.

At that moment The King and Queen and everybody else in the palace woke up. The King and Queen were delighted their daughter

was in love with such a brave Prince and
agreed that they should get married at once.
The Prince and Princess had a beautiful
wedding and a lovely party afterwards.

Everybody came, all except the Wicked Fairy
who had fled the kingdom and was never
seen again.

Meet another girl in Enchantia over the page…

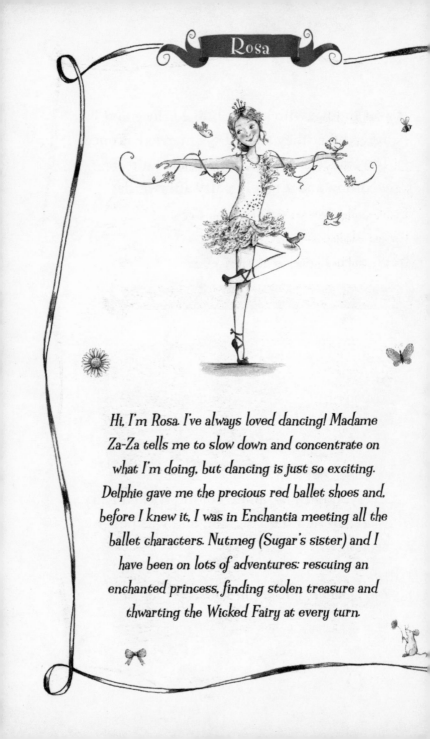

Rosa

Hi, I'm Rosa. I've always loved dancing! Madame Za-Za tells me to slow down and concentrate on what I'm doing, but dancing is just so exciting. Delphie gave me the precious red ballet shoes and, before I knew it, I was in Enchantia meeting all the ballet characters. Nutmeg (Sugar's sister) and I have been on lots of adventures: rescuing an enchanted princess, finding stolen treasure and thwarting the Wicked Fairy at every turn.